WALT DISNEY'S
Bambi

From the Walt Disney Motion Picture *Bambi*
Bambi from the story by Felix Salten
Translated by Whittaker Chambers
Illustrations by the Walt Disney Studio
Adapted by Bob Grant

A GOLDEN BOOK • NEW YORK

Library of Congress Control Number: 2004100450

ISBN: 0-7364-2308-7

www.goldenbooks.com

First Random House Edition 2004

Printed in the United States of America 10

$\mathcal{B}$ambi came into the world in the middle of a thicket, one of those little hidden forest glades which seem to be open but are really screened in on all sides.

The magpie was the first to discover him.

"This is quite an occasion," he said. "It isn't often that a young prince is born. Congratulations!"

Bambi's mother looked up. "Thank you,"
she said quietly. Then she nudged her sleeping
baby gently with her nose. "Wake up," she whispered.
"Wake up!"

The fawn lifted his head and looked around. He
looked frightened and edged closer to his mother's body.
She licked him reassuringly and nudged him again. He
pushed up on his thin hind legs, trying to stand. His
forelegs kept crumpling, but at last they bore his weight
and he stood beside his mother.

"What are you going to name the young prince?"
asked the baby rabbit.

"I'll call him Bambi," the mother answered.

"Bambi," repeated the rabbit. "That's a good name. My name's Thumper." And he hopped away with his mother and sisters.

The little fawn sank down and nestled close to his mother. She licked his spotted red coat softly.

The birds and animals slipped away through the forest, leaving the thicket in peace and quiet.

The forest was beautiful in the summer. The trees stood still under the blue sky, and out of the earth came troops of flowers, unfolding their red, white, and yellow stars.

Bambi liked to follow his mother down the forest paths, so narrow that the thick leafy bushes stroked his flanks as he passed. Sometimes a branch tripped him or a bush tangled about his legs, but always his mother walked easily and surely.

There were friends all along these forest paths. The opossums, hanging by their long tails from the branches of a tree, said, "Hello, Prince Bambi."

As Bambi and his mother reached a little clearing in the forest, they met Thumper and his family.

"Come on, Bambi," said Thumper, "let's play."
And Bambi began to run on his stiff, spindly
legs. Then he saw a family of birds on a low branch.
He stared at them.

"These are birds, Bambi," Thumper said.

"Birds," said Bambi slowly. It was his first word. When he saw a butterfly flutter across the path, he cried, "Bird, bird!" again.

"No, Bambi," said Thumper. "That's not a bird. It's a butterfly."

Then Bambi saw a clump of yellow flowers, and he bounded toward them.

"Butterfly!" he cried.

"No, Bambi," said Thumper. "Flower."

Suddenly he drew back. Out from the bed of flowers came a small black head with two gleaming eyes.

"Flower!" said Bambi.

"That's not a flower," Thumper giggled. "Skunk."

"Flower," said Bambi again.

"The young prince can call me Flower if he wants to," said the skunk. "I don't mind. In fact, I like it."

Bambi had made another friend.

One morning Bambi and his mother walked down a path where the fawn had never been. A few steps more and they would be in a meadow.

"Wait here until I call you," she said. "The meadow is not always safe."

She listened in all directions and called, "Come."

Bambi bounded out. Joy seized him and he leaped into the air, three, four, five times.

"Catch me!" his mother cried, and she bounded ahead.

Bambi started after her. He felt as if he were flying, without any effort.

As he stopped for breath, he saw standing beside him a small fawn.

"Hello," she said, moving nearer to him.

Bambi, shy, bounded away to where he saw his friend, Flower the skunk, playing. He pretended he did not see the new little fawn.

"Don't be afraid, Bambi," his mother said. "That is little Faline; her mother is your Aunt Ena."

Soon Bambi and Faline were racing around hillocks.

Suddenly there was a sound of hoofbeats, and figures came bursting out of the woods. They were the stags.

One of the stags was larger and stronger than all the others. This was the great Prince of the Forest, very brave and wise.

The great stag uttered one dreadful word: "MAN!"

Instantly birds and animals rushed toward the woods. As Bambi and his mother disappeared into the trees, they heard behind them on the meadow loud, roaring noises, terrifying to Bambi's ears.

Later, as Bambi and his mother lay safely in their thicket, his mother explained. "MAN. Bambi—it was MAN in the meadow. He brings danger and death to the forest with his long stick that roars and spurts flames. Someday you will understand."

One morning Bambi woke up shivering with cold. His nose told him there was something strange in the world. When he looked out through the thicket he saw everything covered with white.

"It's snow, Bambi," his mother said. "Go ahead and walk out."

Cautiously Bambi stepped on the surface of the snow and saw his feet sink down in it. The air was calm and the sun on the white snow sparkled. Bambi was delighted.

As he walked, stepping high and carefully, a breeze shifted a branch above him ever so slightly, just enough to tip a heavy load of snow on Bambi's head. He jumped high in the air, startled and frightened, then ran on, licking the snow from his nose. It tasted good—clean and cool.

Thumper was playing on the ice-covered pond, and Bambi trotted gingerly down the slope and out onto the smooth ice, too. His front legs shot forward, his rear legs slipped back and down he crashed! He looked up to see Thumper laughing at him.

He finally lurched to his feet and skidded across the ice dizzily, landing headfirst in a snowbank on the shore.

As he pulled himself out of the drift, he and Thumper heard a faint sound of snoring. Peering down into a deep burrow, they saw the little skunk lying peacefully asleep on a bed of withered flowers.

"Wake up, Flower!" Bambi called.

"Is it spring yet?" Flower asked sleepily.

"No, winter's just beginning," said Bambi.

"I'm hibernating," the little skunk smiled. "Flowers always sleep in the winter." And he dozed off again.

So Bambi learned about winter. It was a difficult time for all the animals in the forest. Food grew scarce. Sometimes Bambi and his mother had to strip bark from trees and eat it.

At last, when it seemed they could find no more to eat, there was a change in the air. Thin sunshine filtered through the bare branches, and the air was a little warmer. That day, too, Bambi's mother dug under the soft snow and found a few blades of pale green grass.

Bambi and his mother were nibbling at the grass when they suddenly smelled MAN. As they lifted their heads, there came a deafening roar like thunder.

"Quick, Bambi," his mother said, "run for the thicket. Don't stop, no matter what happens."

Bambi darted away and heard his mother's footsteps behind him. Then came another roar from MAN's guns. Bambi dashed among the trees in terrified speed. But when he came at last to the thicket his mother was not in sight. He sniffed the air for her smell, listened for her hoofbeats. There was nothing!

Bambi raced out into the forest, calling wildly for his mother. Silently the old stag appeared beside him.

"Your mother can't be with you any more," the stag said. "You must learn to walk alone."

In silence Bambi followed the great stag off through the snow filled forest.

Soon it was spring. Everything was turning green,
and the leaves looked fresh and smiling.

Suddenly Bambi looked up and saw another deer.

"Hello, Bambi," said the other deer. "Don't you remember me? I'm Faline." Bambi stared at her. Faline was now a graceful and beautiful doe.

A strange excitement swept over Bambi. When Faline trotted up and licked his face, Bambi started to dash away. But after a few steps he stopped. Faline dashed into the bushes and Bambi followed.

Suddenly Ronno, a buck with big antlers, stood between Bambi and Faline.

"Stop!" he cried. "Faline is going with me."

Bambi stood still as Ronno nudged Faline down the path. Suddenly he shot forward, and they charged together with a crash.

Again and again they came together, forehead to forehead. Then a prong broke from Ronno's antlers, a terrific blow tore open his shoulder, and he fell to the ground, sliding down a rocky embankment.

As Ronno limped off into the forest, Bambi and Faline walked away through the woods. At night they trotted onto the meadow, where they stood in the moonlight, listening to the east wind and the west wind calling to each other.

Early one morning in the autumn Bambi sniffed the scent of MAN.

The great stag came and said, "Yes, Bambi, it's MAN, with tents and campfires. We must go to the hills."

Bambi ran back to the thicket for Faline. The sounds of MAN and the barking of dogs came closer.

He lunged at the dogs and called, "Run, Faline!"

The roar of a gun crashed almost beside him, but he dashed ahead as a killing pain shot through him.

The old stag appeared and said, "The forest has caught fire from the flames of MAN's campfires. We must go to the river." They plunged into the raging fire, and then fell into cool, rushing water.

Panting and breathless, they struggled onto a safe shore, already crowded with other animals.

With a cry of joy Faline came running to him and gently licked the wound on his shoulder.

Together they stood on the shore, and watched the flames destroy their forest home.

But soon spring came again, and green leaves and grass and flowers covered the scars left by the fire.

Again news went through the forest. "Come along, come to the thicket."

At the thicket, the squirrels and rabbits and birds were peering through the undergrowth at Faline and two spotted fawns.

And not far away was Bambi, the proud father, and the new great Prince of the Forest.